THUNDERBIRDS ARE GO!

UNIVERSAL PICTURES AND STUDIOCANAL PRESENT A WORKING TITLE PRODUCTION A JONATHAN FRAKES FILM "THUNDERBIRDS" BILL PAXTON ANTHONY EDWARDS SOPHIA MYLES AND BEN KINGSLEY CASTING BY MARY SELWAY CDG FIONA WEIR MUSIC BY HANS ZIMMER COSTUME DESIGNER MARIT ALLEN EDITOR MARTIN WALSH A.C.E. PRODUCTION DESIGNER JOHN BEARD DIRECTOR OF PHOTOGRAPHY BRENDAN GALVIN EXECUTIVE PRODUCERS DEBRA HAYWARD LIZA CHASIN PRODUCED BY TIM BEVAN ERIC FELLNER MARK HUFFAM STORY BY PETER HEWITT AND WILLIAM OSBORNE SCREENPLAY BY WILLIAM OSBORNE AND MICHAEL McCULLERS DIRECTED BY JONATHAN FRAKES www.thunderbirdsmovie.com A UNIVERSAL RELEASE

PG PARENTAL GUIDANCE SUGGESTED
SOME MATERIAL MAY NOT BE SUITABLE FOR CHILDREN
INTENSE ACTION SEQUENCES
AND LANGUAGE
For rating reasons, go to www.filmratings.com

Thunderbirds: Thunderbirds Are Go!

THUNDERBIRDS

THUNDERBIRDS ARE GO!

Adapted by Kitty Richards

Based on a motion picture screenplay
written by William Osborne and Michael McCullers

Story by Peter Hewitt and William Osborne

Based on the original television series
"Thunderbirds" © ITC Distribution, LLC

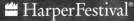

HarperFestival®
A Division of HarperCollinsPublishers

Prologue

In the year 2010, billionaire ex-astronaut Jeff Tracy lost his wife in a tragic accident. Consumed by grief, he took his five sons to an uncharted tropical island to rebuild their lives.

There, in her memory, he built the secret headquarters of International Rescue—an organization dedicated to helping those in need, wherever and whenever disaster strikes. They have come to be known by the name they gave their incredible machines—*Thunderbirds*!

And this is their story. . . .

Chapter One

Thunderbirds 1 and 2 streaked across the Tokyo skyline on their way to save the day, as usual. On the other side of the world, fourteen-year-old Alan Tracy was in trouble, as usual. The stole-your-headmaster's-car-engine-and-hot-wired-it-to-your-scooter-then-went-out-of-control-in-a-race-and-crash-landed-in-the-pond-on-the-front-lawn-of-your-exclusive-boarding-school-soaking-your-already-angry-headmaster kind of trouble. In other words—big trouble. He and his classmates had raced through the woods on souped-up Vespas, and Alan had completely lost control. It had not been a very pretty sight. Worst of all, Alan had lost to a know-it-all classmate. What a bummer.

Also as usual, Alan's best friend, Fermat Hackenbacker, was worried. He pushed his oversized glasses back up the bridge of his nose nervously as he waited to hear what punishment the headmaster had given Alan. "W—w—well, how did it go?" he asked. Fermat had a stutter and it came out whenever he was angry, upset, or anxious. And right now, Fermat was a combination of all three.

Alan gave the good news first. "I'm not going to be expelled . . ." he began.

Fermat looked hopeful.

". . . Till Friday," Alan finished. "Don't worry, it's no big deal."

But it *was* a big deal to Fermat. He took school very seriously—and his best friend was running out of schools to attend. He had *blown up* his last one, for heaven's sake!

Suddenly a boy ran down the hallway. "Turn on the TV!" he yelled as he ran past them. "Turn on the TV! It's the Thunderbirds!"

Alan and Fermat took off after the boy and followed him into the school common room. It was already packed with kids, their eyes glued to the screen. There was an oil rig disaster in the

Bering Strait. The huge rig, about the size of five football fields, was completely ablaze and in danger of total collapse. Six workers were still trapped, clinging to the platform for dear life. The situation looked grim.

That's when *Thunderbird 1*, a swept-wing rocket ship, and *Thunderbird 2*, a massive green rocket, zoomed in for the rescue. The kids cheered.

Alan watched worriedly. His father, Jeff, and his brothers Virgil, Scott, and Gordon were inside. The wind shear was harsh. This would be a most difficult mission. He pushed his way to the front of the room. "Come on, Dad," he muttered to himself.

Everyone watched breathlessly as waves

crashed over the workers and burning debris rained down. *Thunderbird 2* blazed in and hovered above them. Virgil emerged from *Thunderbird 2* with the rescue lines. He carefully targeted the workers and—Yes!— the lines were secure. The workers were all pulled to safety.

Alan's know-it-all classmate piped up. "I bet they bring in *Thunderbird 3* to put out the fire!"

Almost absentmindedly Alan replied, "No, *Thunderbird 3* is only used for extra-orbital missions. They'll probably launch a rocket from *Thunderbird 1*."

The know-it-all kid gave Alan a know-it-all look. "Only an idiot would use a rocket to fight a fire." He sneered. "What makes *you* such a Thunderbird expert anyway?"

Alan was burning up. He opened his mouth, ready to put the kid in his place. "Funny you should ask but . . ."

Fermat stomped on his foot. Alan *knew* he had to keep his connection to the Thunderbirds a secret! "W—w—we've actually read a lot of articles about them," Fermat finished for his friend.

Meanwhile, *Thunderbird 1* streaked toward the blazing structure. A small projectile blasted out of its nose cone. It headed for the flaming column of oil and—*Boom!*—the projectile exploded directly over the well head, enveloping the rig in a cloud of smoke, seawater, and steam.

The fire was extinguished. The Thunderbirds had done it again.

Alan gave the know-it-all kid his very own know-it-all look. A told-you-so look. No doubt about it, Alan knew his stuff.

Just then the headmaster appeared with International Rescue's beautiful undercover agent, Lady Penelope Creighton-Ward. She had come to take Alan and Fermat home to Tracy Island for spring break.

The know-it-all kid stared, open-mouthed, at Lady Penelope. For once he had absolutely nothing to say.

Chapter Two

"Hi, Nosey," Alan said to Lady Penelope's chauffeur, Parker, who stood in front of *FAB 1*, a six-wheeled baby-pink limousine with a glass canopy for a roof. The boys grinned at each other. *FAB 1* wasn't just a car—it flew, too! Alan gave Lady Penelope a grateful look as he got inside. She had bailed him out again. No expulsion for him this time!

Meanwhile, the Thunderbirds dropped the six rescued oil rig workers off at a San Francisco hospital. The Tracys didn't know it, but the disaster was no accident! One of the oil workers was an imposter. He was a big, hulking fellow named Mullion, and he worked for a very evil man known

only as The Hood. Once the Thunderbirds unloaded their passengers, Mullion went to work. He flipped a switch on his belt buckle, and a tiny projectile flew out, smashing into the nose cone of *Thunderbird 2*. It was filled with a liquid tracking solution, which spread onto the rocket. When the Tracys flew home, The Hood would have the exact coordinates for the secret location of Tracy Island!

"Mission complete, *Thunderbird 1*," said Jeff Tracy. "We're good to go."

"F.A.B.," said Scott.

On Tracy Island, Fermat's father, Brains, was anxiously awaiting everyone's arrival. *FAB 1* landed on the island at the same time as *Thunderbirds 1* and *2*. Onaha, the housekeeper, was putting dinner on the table. Alan and Fermat hugged their fathers hello, and everyone sat down for dinner, including Onaha's husband, Kyrano, and their daughter, Tin-Tin.

Alan was really glad to see everyone, but he wasn't enjoying all the jokes his brothers were making at his expense. Luckily, only three of them were there to give him grief. John, his oldest brother, was up in *Thunderbird 5*, a huge space station. He was monitoring disasters around the world.

After dinner, Alan and Fermat decided to go sit in *Thunderbird 1*. Alan accidentally flipped the wrong switch and the cockpit burst into life. His father's face immediately popped up on the screen. Busted! "Come into my office, Alan, now!" his father commanded.

Once again, Alan was in trouble. Huge trouble. He had broken rule number one: Do not start a *Thunderbird* without putting up the anti-detection shield. As a matter of fact, as a Thunderbird in the making, he wasn't even supposed to go anywhere *near* the *Thunderbirds*. Correction—colossal trouble! His father was grounding him for the rest of spring break.

"You put everyone in danger when you act selfishly," Jeff told his youngest son. "Understand?"

Alan clenched his jaw. "I understand," he said.

"I understand you don't want me to be a Thunderbird."

Jeff shook his head. "Bottom line, Alan, you need to grow up."

"Then let me!" Alan shouted, running out of the room.

Tracy Island was quiet. But that would soon change, for The Hood's submarine had arrived

and lay in wait right off Tracy Island Beach. It was time for some last-minute instructions. The Hood addressed his team. The brawn, Mullion, and the brains, Transom, a female computer genius with thick glasses, listened closely.

"The Thunderbirds' purpose is to rescue," said The Hood. "All we need to do is give them a victim."

Their chosen victim was Alan's oldest brother,

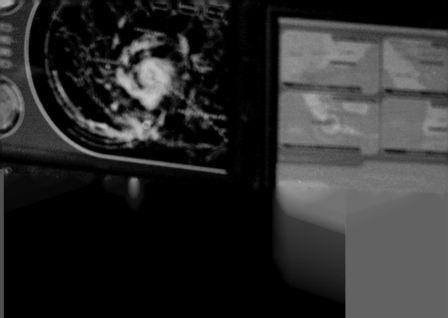

John, in *Thunderbird 5*. Transom hit a button and launched a missile at the space station. *Boom!* It was a direct hit.

"*Thunderbird 5* to Tracy Island! Mayday! Mayday!" shouted John.

Brains burst into Jeff's office and sat behind the main console. "Switching to command and control center," he said. Instantly the office was transformed. The furniture folded away into the floor, the huge wooden desk was replaced by a massive control console, giant screens and banks of computer equipment popped up through the floor and down from the ceiling, and huge steel blast shutters slid across the windows.

Jeff, Virgil, Scott, and Gordon rushed into the room and took their places in front of their portraits, which lined one of the walls. Instantly they were in their flight suits.

"Thunderbirds are *go*!" shouted Jeff.

The wall flipped back and they were gone, leaving Alan behind.

Chapter Three

Brains turned back to the monitor and his jaw dropped in disbelief. It couldn't be—could it? This was a top secret location! But there it was, right in front of his eyes—a submarine had just surfaced in their lagoon! He hit the "intruder alert" button, and the command center transformed back into an office. And just in time, too, because Transom had activated a communications blackout. Brains immediately lost contact with *Thunderbird 3*.

Alan, Fermat, and Tin-Tin were standing on the beach when the submarine surfaced. "Run!" they yelled. They made their way to the control room through the ventilation system, then

watched through the eyeholes in the portraits on the wall. They couldn't believe their eyes as they saw The Hood, with only the power of his mind, force Brains to activate the control switch to change the office back into a command center. Onaha and Kyrano were captured, too.

Things were not looking good at all.

Thunderbird 3 rocketed into space to rescue John. The station was starting to spin out of control. *Thunderbird 5* had lost all power and the generators were down. *Thunderbird 3* docked, and Jeff, Virgil, Scott, and Gordon scrambled inside. There were fires to put out and oxygen systems to repair—and no time to lose.

"Let's move!" shouted Jeff.

Then alarms blared. The situation was way too dangerous. It was time to get out.

"Back to *Thunderbird 3*, now!" called Jeff.

Scott punched in a sequence of numbers on the door panel. Nothing happened. The locking mechanism was jammed.

Suddenly The Hood's voice rang out, and his face appeared on a viewscreen. "Attention,

Thunderbird 5," he began. "As you can see, I have taken over your facilities. You no longer control your operational systems.

"You can call me The Hood," he continued. "Now listen, Mr. Tracy. We won't be negotiating. I'm going to use the *Thunderbirds* to rob the largest banks in the world, starting with the Bank of London. The world's monetary system will be thrown into chaos—and the Thunderbirds held responsible."

Jeff shook his head in disbelief. "But the Thunderbirds were supposed to save lives, not cause chaos."

The Hood narrowed his eyes. "You're only alive because I want you to see me destroy in ten hours what it took you ten years to build. An eye for an eye, Mr. Tracy."

Jeff was confused. "I don't know what you're talking about."

"Perhaps you've forgotten me, but surely you remember saving the life of my brother, Kyrano. You left me to die that day. Well, you may have broken my body, but you have no idea how powerful my mind has become. Now you will suffer as

I have suffered, waiting for a rescue that will never come."

Tin-Tin stared. Did that mean she was *related* to this criminal?

Suddenly Fermat sneezed, and Mullion realized they were in the duct. He punched through the wall and grabbed Alan. Thinking fast, Tin-Tin bit Mullion's hand. With a cry of pain, he let go. The three kids made their escape. They each had one thought on their minds—their parents. Alan's dad was somewhere out in space. Fermat and Tin-Tin's folks were held captive in a giant refrigerator. With their families in The Hood's evil clutches, it was up to *them* to save the day.

Back on *Thunderbird 5*, the boys had managed to wire in the oxygen scrubber to the emergency batteries. But it only gave them four short hours to breathe. The Thunderbirds were in terrible danger.

Things weren't looking so good down on earth, either. The kids raced to the silo that housed *Thunderbird 2*. Transom spotted them on the monitor, and the doors slammed shut. They were trapped! When Mullion arrived to capture them, Fermat and Tin-Tin went on the attack with the *Firefly*, an eight-wheeled fire-fighting truck topped with a foam cannon. When the pressure was upped to 500 psi, an incredibly high setting, it let out a *serious* burst of congealing foam. Meanwhile, Alan blasted a hole through the door with the *Thunderizer*, a powerful machine that shot charged particles. They were out!

They ran like the wind to the service tunnel entrance. As Alan punched in the code to enter, he looked up and gasped. The Hood was staring at him from the other side of the safety glass!

"You can run if you want," The Hood said. He gazed at Alan. "Were you surprised to hear what your father did to me? Realizing our parents aren't perfect is frightening. Why did he build these magnificent machines? Do you suppose it was guilt, Alan? Because he let your mother die?"

Alan was stunned.

"Open the door, Alan," The Hood commanded. Alan tried to run, but his legs wouldn't move. "Open the door!" The Hood said again. Finally Alan managed to tear himself away. He ran over

to Fermat and Tin-Tin, and they raced to the base of *Thunderbird 1*. But it was no use. They were surrounded.

It can't end like this, Alan thought to himself. He looked around the room wildly. And then he had an idea. He secretly loaded a rock into his stone skimmer and aimed it at a large red button on the wall. The steel floor beneath *Thunderbird 1* shot open. The kids fell down into a blast duct.

This gave Mullion a horribly evil idea. "Transom, fire up *Thunderbird 1* and set to broil!" he thundered.

Chapter Four

Yikes! The kids flew down the air duct, closely followed by a colossal ball of flame. Just as they were about to be charbroiled, they shot out of the bottom and into the ocean.

Once they made it to land and wrung out their clothes, Alan told his friends his idea. "The Hood must have overridden *Thunderbird 5*'s systems using the main computer in the control room. All we need to do is reprogram that computer."

But how would they get to the computer without The Hood crushing them like bugs?

"I m—m—might have an idea," Fermat spoke up. "Data from Tracy Island is sent to *Thunderbird 5* via satellite. There is a miniscule possibility that if we reach the island's satellite station we

could hack into it and give control back to *Thunderbird 5*."

The kids looked at each other and sighed. To get to the satellite station they would have to go through the jungle—which had always been off-limits. It would be dangerous, but what was at stake was way too important.

Fermat, Alan, and Tin-Tin worked their way through the jungle. It was steep. It was thick. It was *exhausting*. And it was full of creepy, crawly, hideous bugs. Sweaty, grossed out, and a little bit scared, they trekked along. Suddenly Tin-Tin looked at Alan and froze. There was an Androctonus scorpion on his shoulder! "P—p—point zero two five milligrams of its venom are fatal," said Fermat. Just as the creature was about to strike, Tin-Tin's eyes flashed. The scorpion flew off of Alan's shoulder and landed on the ground.

Alan and Fermat stared at Tin-Tin. Apparently superpowers ran in her family.

Thinking the kids were now yesterday's news, Transom, Mullion, and The Hood entered *Thunderbird 2*'s cockpit, ready to put phase two of their evil plan into action. Transom hit a row of switches and the lights began to flicker. Suddenly

all the lights in the cockpit blinked red and an alarm began to buzz. Transom reached over, opened a panel, and discovered that something was wrong—terribly wrong.

The guidance processor was missing. And they weren't going anywhere without it.

"It's the children," The Hood said softly. "They have it."

Fermat reached into his pocket and felt for the guidance processor. He pulled it out. Alan jumped up and grabbed it. "This is the guidance processor from *Thunderbird 2*. It can't take off without it. Fermat, you're a genius."

He, Alan, and Tin-Tin had finally made it in one piece to the top of Tracy Island. They stood in front of an array of satellite dishes, watching as Fermat spliced wires inside a large service box. At one point he had to use a crystal from Tin-Tin's necklace along with a wire from Alan's orthodontic retainer (given rather unwillingly) to solder the circuit board back together. Finally it was up and running.

"You're the man, Fermat!" he congratulated himself.

An image suddenly appeared on the screen.

They squinted and could just make out Jeff and the Tracy boys. The heat exchanger on *Thunderbird 5* had blown and the situation was getting worse by the minute.

"Dad!" Alan called. "I'm at the satellite relay station with Fermat and Tin-Tin. We're going to hack into the computer system and return control of *Thunderbird 5* to you."

Transferring the data was going to take a couple of minutes. Fermat began hacking away.

Unfortunately, back at the compound, the control board beeped, alerting Transom to the kids' location.

The screen began to break up. "They're on to us!" called Fermat. "W—w—we're being jammed!"

Alan took a deep breath and delivered the bad news to his dad. "They're jamming our signal," he explained. "We're going to lose you. Don't worry; I'll take care of everything."

"Negative!" said Jeff. "It's too dangerous. Follow emergency procedure—wait for Lady Penelope at the rendezvous point."

And then the screen went black.

The kids didn't even have a minute to think. Mullion raced up on a roaring beach buggy. They sprinted back into the jungle, but the fierce off-road vehicle was right behind them. They raced to the scrap yard where Alan found a beat-up hoversled.

"It's our ticket out of here," said Alan. "Unless you have a better idea."

"Let's wait for Lady Penelope, like your Dad said," Tin-Tin suggested.

"Great idea," said Alan sarcastically. "Let's sit around and wait to get caught. We have to do something now. Right, Fermat?"

"Actually, I agree with Tin-Tin," Fermat said. "I don't think it's s—s—safe."

Alan stared at his best friend in shock. He couldn't believe Fermat wasn't backing him up. "You don't think anything is s—s—safe," he said mockingly.

Fermat stared at Alan as if he had just been slapped in the face. "Just because I st—stutter doesn't mean I'm wrong," he said. "If we're a team, we should make decisions as a team."

"Do you guys want to stop and take a vote, or do you want to get out of here?" Alan demanded. "Because I'm going." He turned and walked over to the hoversled. After a beat, Fermat followed.

"You know, you can be a real jerk sometimes,"

Tin-Tin said to Alan as she joined them. Alan got on in the front of the sled, and Tin-Tin and Fermat got into the sidecar. Alan kickstarted the hover-sled, and they began a wild ride through the jungle, Fermat and Tin-Tin taking the worst of it.

Suddenly Mullion was right behind them on the beach buggy.

"Hang on!" shouted Alan, accelerating. If they could make it past the rocks ahead, they could leave old Mullion behind.

"You're going too fast!" Fermat shouted. Ignoring his friend, Alan engaged a final burst of speed, and shot between two jagged rocks.

"What did I tell you guys?" he said gleefully, turning around to smile at them and accept their congratulations. But they—and their sidecar— were gone. Alan watched with dread as his two friends were captured by Mullion.

"I *can* be a real jerk sometimes," he said to himself.

Chapter Five

Slam! The refrigerator door banged shut as Tin-Tin and Fermat were thrown inside with the other captives. While seeing their parents was really nice, it definitely wasn't the happiest of family reunions. Everything was up to Alan now.

And out in space on *Thunderbird 5*, things were getting worse. The ship had begun to vibrate wildly, rivets popping from the steel super-structure. The temperature was rising rapidly, and gravity was further deteriorating. It was getting as hot as blazes. "Hang in there, guys," said Virgil. "Re-entry into atmosphere in thirty-seven minutes."

"Oxygen's out in thirty, so we won't feel a thing," Scott scoffed.

"Stop it," commanded Jeff.

"Come on, Dad, the situation's hopeless," said Gordon.

Jeff shook his head. "I don't know what that word means. We've still got time, and we've got people on the ground working for us."

"Alan?" said Gordon. "He's just a kid."

"But he's a *Tracy*," Jeff said.

Alone, Alan traveled back to the compound. Hidden in the bushes, he watched as Parker and Lady Penelope put up a good fight before they were captured, too, thanks to The Hood's powers. But Alan noticed that The Hood was slowing down. "Using his powers must make him weak," he whispered.

Suddenly The Hood spoke. "How are you, Alan?" he said. He signaled to Mullion, and the big man kicked the back of Parker's head. Parker cried out in pain.

"You can make it stop, Alan," said The Hood. "You have something that belongs to me."

Alan knew he was beaten. Before Mullion could hurt Parker again, Alan scrambled forward. He pulled out the guidance processor that Fermat had given him and threw it into the bushes. But The Hood was able to make the processor float right into his hand. Transom tossed Alan into the deep freeze along with the others.

"How long do Jeff and the boys have?" Lady Penelope asked.

Fermat calculated they had three minutes.

Alan's stomach sank. "We've got to get to the control room and reprogram that computer!" he cried.

They needed to get out and they needed to get out *now*. Glancing up at the ceiling vent, Lady Penelope noticed that it was coated with built-up ice. Removing one of her wickedly high-heeled shoes, she took careful aim. An icicle fell and sliced through Parker's ropes. He quickly untied everyone and picked the lock on the freezer door. They were free! But was there enough time to save Jeff and the Tracy boys?

"Less than a minute left!" Fermat shouted. They raced for the command and control center. Brains and Fermat desperately worked together to regain control of the space station.

"I'm in! I'm in!" Fermat shouted. "I just need someone on their end to confirm the access protocol."

But was anyone—*gulp*—alive to answer?

"*Thunderbird 5*, come in. Mr. Tracy, can you hear me?" Brains pleaded.

Nothing but static.

"Twenty seconds until reentry," Fermat warned.

"Darn it, Jeff, wake up!" Brains yelled.

Were they too late?

Chapter Six

Silence.

And then, suddenly, someone spoke. "I think that's the first time you've ever called me by my first name," Jeff's hoarse voice answered. "Thanks for waking me, Brains."

Jeff and the boys were okay! Gravity was restored and they could breathe again! And so, finally, could Alan.

It was time to go after The Hood, who had blasted off to London in *Thunderbird 2* to rob the Bank of England. But *Thunderbird 3* had lost a booster. They'd never make it in time.

"Let me go after The Hood!" Alan pleaded with his father. "He'll destroy everything you built, everything the Thunderbirds stand for!"

Jeff shook his head. "Negative. It's too dangerous."

"I can do this," Alan said. "You know I can." Then he stopped. "What am I saying?" He turned to Tin-Tin and Fermat. "*We* can do this," he corrected himself.

Jeff relented. "We'll meet you there, son," he said with a nod. "Thunderbirds are *go*!"

Thunderbird 2 had just arrived in London. The huge ship had barely made it under the Tower Bridge, had shattered a thousand windows in the County Hall Building, and had made what would be a most non-regulation landing in the Jubilee

Gardens, scattering hundreds of bystanders, who just barely escaped with their lives as they ran for safety. Everyone stared in shock. The Thunderbirds were supposed to save the day—not put lives in danger! Next, the *Mole*—a gigantic drilling machine twice the size of a locomotive—emerged from *Thunderbird 2*, crushing picnic tables in its way.

"Due to a change in management," Mullion thundered over the PA system, "The Thunderbirds no longer rescue. We destroy!"

As the terrified crowd watched, open-mouthed, the *Mole* rose up. Its teeth started to spin and it began to bite into the earth, digging down, down, down.

From inside the *Mole*, The Hood said, "Set a course for the vault."

Transom studied the readouts. "Sir, if we continue on our present course, we'll sever the monorail's subterranean supports. Shall I correct our position?"

The Hood looked at her coldly. "Stay on

course," he commanded.

"But, sir, we'll cause a major disaster," she protested.

The Hood smiled an evil smile. "We won't. The Thunderbirds will."

As the onlookers watched in shock, the mono-

rail began to collapse. The passengers screamed. They were headed toward certain death.

Thunderbird 1 came in for a landing alongside *Thunderbird 2* and surveyed the situation.

"That cable won't hold much longer," said Lady Penelope. Alan, Tin-Tin, and Fermat fired up *Thunderbird 2* while Lady Penelope took off after The Hood.

Alan coolly scanned the scene. "Okay, Fermat," he said. "I'm going to need you to fire a grappling rocket at the support beam."

Fermat started to stutter. "B—b—but I've n—n—never d—d—"

Alan looked his friend in the eye. "Fermat, real bravery is being scared and doing the right thing anyway. The Thunderbirds need you right now. *I* need you."

Fermat pushed his glasses firmly up on the bridge of his nose and nodded.

That's when Alan leaned over and added, "And don't mess it up or everyone'll get killed. No pressure."

Fermat gulped. This was the challenge of a lifetime.

Chapter Seven

Fermat took a deep breath and aimed.

Bang! Direct hit!

The grapple was in place. *Thunderbird 2* slowly began to pull the monorail upright. The crowd cheered. Then suddenly a crack appeared. With a horrifying snap, the rail split in two! The carriage rolled down the broken rail and slid right into the river! Water began pouring in through the doors and windows. What would they do now?

In the *Thunderbird 2* cockpit, Alan made a decision. "I'm going down in *Thunderbird 4*," he stated, leaving Fermat and Tin-Tin in *Thunderbird 2*.

Thunderbird 4 was lowered down and then shot into the river. In order to cut the monorail free, Alan needed Fermat to fire another line. But

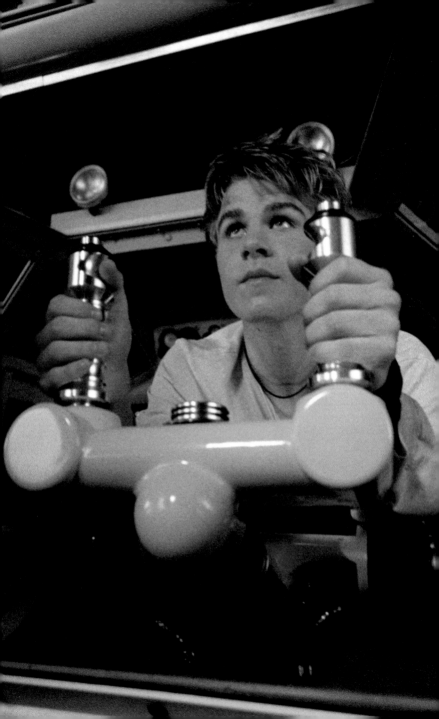

the water was too murky and Fermat was afraid he would hit the passengers.

"I'll do it manually," volunteered Tin-Tin. She took a deep breath, dove underwater, and attached the cable to the carriage.

Alan started to cut through the twisted metal.

Just as *Thunderbird 3* landed on the banks of the Thames, piloted by Jeff and the boys, bubbles began rising to the surface. The monorail car popped up. Fermat, Tin-Tin, and Alan's first rescue was a success!

The crowd cheered.

"Glad you could finally join us, Dad," Alan said smugly.

"Hey, don't go getting cocky after one mission," Jeff said. "We've still got a dangerous situation here. I need you boys to close down this accident scene," he said to the rest of his sons. He turned to Alan and Tin-Tin. "Get Fermat and meet us at *Thunderbird 2.*"

Meanwhile, inside the Bank of England, The Hood, Mullion, and Transom had activated the electromagnetic pulse to disable the bank's security systems. Next they tore the doors off safety deposit boxes with a punch gun and emptied the drawers of people's precious valuables.

Soon they began to move in for the kill.

Alan had an important question to ask his father. "That stuff The Hood said . . . about you leaving him to die. . . . He was lying, right?

Jeff took a deep breath. "No. It's not as simple as that, Alan. You can't always save everyone. The Hood kept his mine workers in chains. They couldn't even run when the tunnels started to collapse. We had to seal the shaft or hundreds more people would have died. So I made a choice." He sighed. "It doesn't matter how hard you try, how brave you are. It doesn't even matter if it's someone you love, or if you'd give up your life in a second to save hers. You just can't save everyone." He had a faraway look in his eyes.

Alan knew exactly what his dad was talking about.

"What was Mom like?" he asked.

His father smiled. "She was F.A.B."

Jeff, Alan, and Tin-Tin got into *Thunderbird 1* and headed straight for the bank, leaving the other Tracys behind to take care of clean-up.

From the depths of the bank vaults, The Hood sensed a presence. "The Thunderbirds," he said. "They're here." He looked at Mullion and Transom. "Kill them all."

Jeff left the kids with Parker and ran off to help Lady Penelope. A moment later, Alan

distracted Parker and raced off to find The Hood. Alan knew The Hood's weakness. He knew he could defeat him.

Lady Penelope was in a giant room. The *Mole*, which The Hood had used to break into the bank, sat in a pile of rubble in the corner. There were two huge cages at either end of the room, each filled with gold bullion and other valuables. Lady Penelope was tied to the bars of one of the cages. Jeff ran toward her but stopped when he saw The Hood emerging from the shadows.

"Did you save them all this time, Jeff?" The Hood said in a mocking tone. "Or did you leave someone behind?"

Jeff stared at The Hood. "I didn't make you what you are," he said.

"It's not *me* you have to convince," The Hood replied, nodding toward Alan, who had just run into the room out of breath.

"Leave my son out of this," Jeff said. He charged at The Hood, but was no match for his powers. Jeff was jerked backward, lost his balance, and flew thirty feet through the air, straight into the cage containing Lady Penelope. He landed in a heap, and the cage door slammed shut behind him with a mighty clang.

"Dad!" Alan cried.

The Hood turned around and faced Alan. Alan noticed the villain was breathing heavily.

"I'm disappointed, Alan," said The Hood. "I thought we were kindred spirits."

Alan narrowed his eyes at The Hood. "Well, we're not," he declared. "You're a creep. And I'm Jeff Tracy's son."

"You certainly are," said The Hood. And he did not mean that as a compliment.

With a mere wave of his hand, The Hood caused Alan to fly across the room and slam into a wall. The Hood flipped into the air and landed on a nearby catwalk. Despite his pain, Alan was focused enough to notice that The Hood had stumbled to one knee before he stood up.

The Hood stared down at Alan, who was still crumpled on the floor.

"You want so badly to walk in daddy's foot-steps," The Hood said mockingly. He lifted his hand, and Alan rose five feet into the air. Alan struggled mightily as he began to choke.

"Did you really think you could challenge me?" The Hood asked, dropping Alan back down dangerously close to some electrical wires. The Hood stumbled, then caught himself.

Jeff couldn't stand to watch his youngest son take the wrath of his own enemy. "Alan, just run!" he called.

But as usual, Alan had a plan. "He's getting weaker," he said. "He can't last much longer."

"Neither can you!" Jeff said. He had a good point.

Alan watched as The Hood made his way to the cockpit of the *Mole*. With the last of his remaining strength, Alan began to climb up the *Mole*'s sharp teeth to beat him there.

The Hood used *his* last bit of energy to wave a finger at the *Mole*. It roared to life. Jeff winced. His youngest son was about to be ground into hamburger meat! But Alan managed to nimbly leap from tooth to tooth and then launched himself in the air toward the gantry. He just managed to grab on with one hand. He hung above the gnawing gears of the *Mole*, which were now up to full speed. Above him loomed The Hood.

"I'm glad you could be here to see this, Jeff," The Hood said mockingly. He lifted his foot, ready to step on Alan's hand and send him plummeting. Jeff slammed into the side of the cage, totally helpless.

"Good-bye, Alan," The Hood said softly.

Chapter Eight

"Noooooooo!" cried Tin-Tin when she ran into the room and saw Alan dangling above the *Mole*. She stretched out her arms, and her eyes flashed. She created a huge wave of force that spread out and flipped the gantry backward onto its track. Alan was now up on top. The Hood stumbled backward and slipped off the catwalk, barely managing to grab the rail with one hand. Now *he* was the one dangling over the *Mole*'s chattering teeth. His grip was weakening. Any second now he would be a goner.

Alan stood above him.

"Leave me, Alan!" The Hood wailed. "Leave me to die like your father did!"

Alan seemed to be considering the idea.

Suddenly The Hood lost his grip. But Alan reached out with lightning-quick reflexes and grabbed his enemy's wrist before he could fall.

"I don't want to save your life," Alan said slowly. "But it's what we do."

Chapter Nine

Dinner was ready. Alan and his brothers climbed out of the pool. Jeff looked at his boys proudly. Another job well done.

"Tonight was a very special night," Jeff said. "There were moments when I didn't think any of us would see it." He paused. "But we did it because of three incredibly special people." He looked at Alan, Tin-Tin, and Fermat. "The world needs the Thunderbirds—and the Thunderbirds need you." He pinned a Thunderbirds wing emblem to each of their shirts. The three friends stared down at the wings, too overcome with emotion to speak.

Suddenly the ringing of a cell phone broke the

moment. Jeff reached into his jacket pocket and answered it.

"Madame President?" he said. "Of course. Straight away."

Moments later, Jeff was sitting behind his desk, and the boys lined up under their portraits.

"Thunderbirds are *go*!" Jeff shouted.

The wall flipped back and the Thunderbirds—John, Gordon, Scott, Virgil, and now, Alan—disappeared, off on another mission to save the world.